mrs Jimenez

What does it mean?

What does it mean?

SAD

by Sylvia Root Tester
illustrated by Nancy Inderieden

ELGIN, ILLINOIS 60120

Distributed by Childrens Press, 1224 West Van Buren Street, Chicago, Illinois 60607.

Library of Congress Cataloging in Publication Data

Tester, Sylvia Root.
  Sad.

  (What does it mean?)
  SUMMARY: A child talks about how she feels when her pet dog dies and about other times when people are sad.
  1. Sadness—Juvenile literature.   2. Death—Psychological aspects—Juvenile literature.   [1. Sadness.   2. Death]
I. Inderieden, Nancy.   II. Title.
BF575.G7T47   152.4   79-26252
ISBN 0-89565-112-2

6

It's hard to keep going
when you feel bad,
and today, all day long,
I've been feeling
sad!

You see, Mr. Chips died.
He got sick Saturday.
Oh, I hated to see him
feeling that way.

It made me so

It hurt me so!

We were going
to Grandma's,

but Mr. Chips couldn't go!
Why, he couldn't even
go along for the ride.
I had to leave him
on his bed inside.

Mom took him to the vet
while I was away.
He died, and they buried
him that same day.

Dad told me later.
That's when I cried.
I wanted to find
a good place to hide.

Mom says it's O.K.
to feel that bad.
Everyone does
sometimes.

Everyone feels sad
when friends are
hurt...

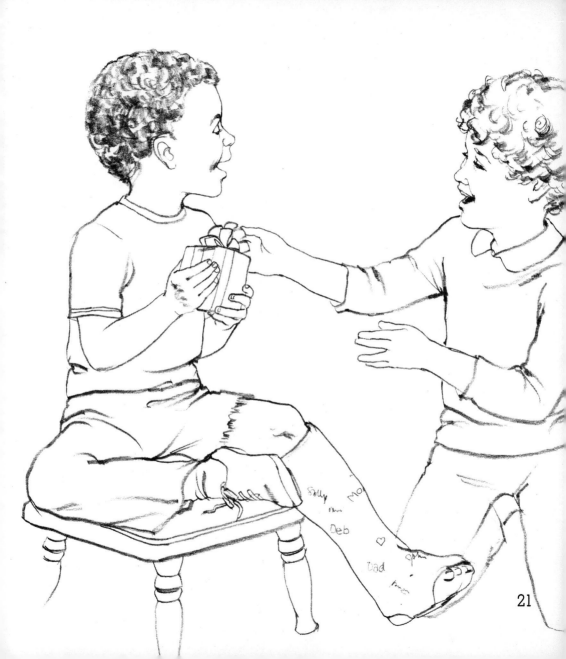

or move away...

when people die...

or when people say,
"We're getting a
divorce!"...

or when
good
friends
fight.

When these things happen,
people don't feel right.

When sad things
happen, there's one
thing to do...